UNDERSTANDING TOMAS GÖSTA TRANSTRÖMER

A CRITICAL JOURNEY THROUGH THE WORKS OF NOBEL LAUREATE

BY

BAIJU KRISHNAN

ISBN 978-93-5438-592-6

© Baiju Krishnan 2021

Published in India 2020 by Pencil

A brand of

One Point Six Technologies Pvt. Ltd.

123, Building J2, Shram Seva Premises,

Wadala Truck Terminal, Wadala (E)

Mumbai 400037, Maharashtra, INDIA

E connect@thepencilapp.com

W www.thepencilapp.com

DISCLAIMER: *The opinions expressed in this book are those of the authors and do not purport to reflect the views of the Publisher.*

Author biography

BAIJU KRISHNAN

Sreenilayam

Kunnathur East PO

Kunnathur, Kollam Dist

Kerala state,

Pin: 690540

baijukletters@yahoo.com

Mr. Baiju Krishnan is presently a research scholar pursuing a Ph.D. in English course from Dravidian University, Kuppam, Andhra Pradesh, India. The author has completed his Master of Arts in English Studies course from the prestigious Central University of Tamil Nadu, Thiruvarur, Tamil Nadu, India and did his Bachelor of Arts in English Language and Literature course in the University of Kerala, Thiruvanathapuram, Kerala, India. In addition to this the author holds a Master of Philosophy in English course from Dravidian University, Kuppam, Andhra Pradesh, India. Further, the author has received an endowment for becoming the topper in English subject at the intermediate level. He has also published papers and articles in journals and book chapters with the presentation of same in several seminars, conferences and workshops of both national and international level. Holding several degrees from different Universities, he is as enthusiastic to learn, research and teach English. His area of specialization includes Film and Literature, Indian English Writing, Gender Studies and Postmodern Literature

Contents

Epigraph

"It is still beautiful to hear the heart beat but often the shadow seems more real than the body."

- Tomas Gösta Tranströmer

DEDICATED TO MY BELOVED PARENTS

I would like to dedicate this book to my beloved Mother Late Shrimati. BhavaniRamakrishnan and my Father Shri.Ramakrishnan M.O.

Preface

"A Critical Journey through the Works of Nobel Laureate: Tomas GöstaTranströmer", is an account of his enormous contributions to literature and his achievements. Transtromer is one of the acclaimed literary debuts of the decade. He was interested in nature and music that has informed a major part of his production. He has shifted towards a smaller format and a higher degree of concentration. His poetry has grown and he was now been translated into more than 50 languages. His work influenced poets around the globe particularly in North America. His famous works are Secret along the Way, Half Finished Heaven, Selected Poems, & Sorrow Gondola.

Transtromer's condensed and translucent images give us fresh access to reality. His works paint simple pictures from everyday life and nature. His profound impact on popular music and American culture is marked by lyrical compositions of extra ordinary poetic power. His most famous works include 'Windows and Stones' in which he depicts the theme from his many travels and 'Baltic's' from 1974.His works are characterized by economy and his style is so simple as to make most words seem vain and superfluous.

His works lie within, and further develops, modernist and expressionist or surrealistic language of the 20th century poetry. Transtromer has described his poems as "Meeting places" where dark and light; interior and exterior collide to give a sudden connection with the world. His love for nature and music guided his writings; gradually his poems become darker, probing essential questions of life, death and disease. His poetry is musical and multilayered.

I hope the present book will serve a useful purpose, and will be immensely useful to literature students. It is hoped that this book will contribute well in understanding Tomas GöstaTranströmer

Acknowledgements 1

First of all, I take the opportunity to express my gratitude to my family. I would like to dedicate this book to my beloved Mother Late Shrimati. BhavaniRamakrishnan. I would like to thank my beloved Father Shri. Ramakrishnan M.O, for his endurance and endless support. Without his encouragement, I would have never imagined to publish a book.

In the preparation and completion of this work, I am deeply indebted to Dr. Y. Joy, Principal of Don Bosco College, Kottiyam, Kerala (Formerly HOD, Department of English, St Cyril's College, Adoor).

I am thankful to all honourable faculty members who had taught and guided me through my B.A. and M.A. courses. Without them, I would not have made it this far. At this moment of accomplishment, last but not the least I would like to thank my teachers: Ms. Sherly Samuel (Thapovan Public School), Late Ms. Manju (VGSSAHSS), Dr. Susan Alexander, Associate Professor, St Cyril's College, Adoor, Dr. Nisha Mathew, Assistant Professor, St Cyril's College, Adoor, Late Prof. P. Rajani, CUTN, Late Dr. Lakshman, CUTN, Dr. Nirmal Selvamony, CUTN, Dr. Jayaraman, CUTN, Dr. Geetha, CUTN and Dr. K. V. Raghupathi, CUTN.

I especially express my sincere gratitude to Prof. Ch. A. Rajendra Prasad, Head, Department of English and

Communications, Dravidian University, Kuppam for his
support and kindness.

-BAIJU KRISHNAN

Introduction

ABOUT THE BOOK

The introductory part is about Transtromer's early life and career, his publications and his experiences during his literary life. It also discusses about his achievements. The second chapter deals with his major works and its literary features. A wide study of his major works is included here. The concluding part throws light upon the themes and style of his works. Transtromer's works are unique and understanding and of universal value. The present book presents in simple and lucid language. This book is especially written for the students from the literature background.

Chapter One - Introduction - Tomas Gösta Tranströmer

The present book entitled, "A Critical Journey through the works of Nobel Lauerete: Tomas GöstaTranströmer" is an attempt to probe into the details of the works of that great personality. Tomas Transtromer is the Nobel Prize winner in literature 2011. He was born in 15th April, 1931.His mother Helmy was a school teacher and father Gosta Transtomer was a journalist. He completed his graduation in 1950 at Sodra Latin grammar school. After that he took BA in Literature, History and Poetics, the history of religion and psychology in 1956 at Stockholm University.

After finished his scholastic investigations and academic studies he was utilized as right hand at the organization for psychometrics at Stockholm University in 1957. Between 1960 and 1966 he functioned as an analyst at Roxtuna, a youth remedial office close to Lingoping. He took a position at the work market foundation in vastero in 1980. In 1990 he endured a stroke that left him generally unfit to talk.

He published numerous poems in journals. In 1954, he published *Dikter* (17 Poems)- One of the most acclaimed proficiency presentations of the decade. Effectively evident was the interest in nature and music that has educated a significant part regarding his creation. He combined his remaining among the critics and different perusers as one of the main artists of his age.

His famous works are '*HemligheterPavagen*' (*Secrets along the way*) (1958), '*Den HalvFardigahimlen*' (*The Half-Finished Heaven*) (1962) and '*Klangeroch spar* '(Bells and Tracks) (1966), and *Författarförlaget* (Paths) (1973).

His poetry collection Ostersjoar (1974; *Balatics*, 1975) gathers fragments of a family chronicle from Runmaro island in the stockholm archipelago, where his maternal grandfather was a pilot and where Transtomer has spend many summers since boyhood. His reminiscences from growing up in the 1930s and 40s are collected in a prose memoir, *MinnenaSerMig* (*Memories Look at Me*) (1993) and *Sorgegondolen* (1996; *The sorrow Gondola*, 1997) and *Denstoragatan* (2004; *The Great Enigma*, 2006). Transtromer has shifted towards as even smaller format and a higher degree of concentration.

He was presented in the US by translator Robert Bly as ahead of schedule as the 1960s. Since then, international interest in his verse has developed and he was currently been translated into more than fifty dialects. He has occasionally published his own translations of verse in other languages. An assortment entitled, *Tolkningar* (interpretations) was published in 1999.Transtromer has portrayed his poems as "meeting places", where dim and light, interior and outside crash to give an abrupt association with the world, history or ourselves. As indicated by the artist, "The language matches in step with the executioners; therefore we must get a new language".

His most well known works include the 1966 '*Windows and Stones*', in which he portrays the men from his numerous movements and 'bal-tics' from 1974. His works impacted artists around the world, especially in North America. The 80-year-old was regarded for a standard of verse which is implanted with similitude's and pictures from the idea of his local land and which investigates wide topics like profound quality, reality, solitude, and reclamation.

In 2007, the Griffin Trust for excellence in poetry gave the Swedish artist a life time achievement award. His love for nature and music guided for his writing. Gradually, Transtromer's poems become darker, probing essential questions of life, death and disease. He used blank verse in '*17 Dikter*'. After that he began to experiment with meter, but mostly wrote poems in free verse. Since the 1950s with American poet Robert Bly, who translated many of his works into English, Transtromer has had a close friendship. In 2001, Transtromers' Bonniers, a swedish publishing house published the correspondence between the two writers in book '*Air mail*'.

Earlier this year, Bonniers released a collection of his works between 1954 and 2004 to celebrate the poets 80th birthday. The Swedish Academy, which decides the winner of Nobel Prize, said it was recognizing him as "thought his condensed, translucent images, he gives us fresh access to reality". This is not the first time that he was born a top literature prize. He won the Neustadt International Prize for literature in 1990, as well as Bonner Award for poetry, Germany's Petrarch prize, Bellman Prize, The Swedish Academy's Nordiac Prize, The Swedish Award from the international poetry Forum, the Oevradlids prize, and August prize.

His poetry collections are filled with imagination and emotion, but at the same time is loaded with the un-experience making his work now and again both muddling and refreshing. Scandinavia's most renowned living poet, Transtromer has been known as an expert of Mysticism who frequently presents a fantasy like awareness in which time shows to consider dismemberment of the connection between the internal identity and the encompassing world. His verse has a modernist, associative and outwardly reminiscent way to deal with language, arranged around a significantly that has been called 'Jungian' (perhaps not in every case precisely).

Transtromer's standing position in the English literary world owes a lot to his companionship with American writer Robert Bly, who has deciphered, translated quite a bit of his works in English. Transtromer's work paints basic pictures from regular daily existence and nature. In his equal profession as an artist and analyst, he additionally worked with the disabled, convicts and medication addicts while, at a similar time, creating an enormous group of idyllic work. He is an unpretentiously exceptional author whose style is so basic as to make most words appear to be vain and unnecessary. In interpretation a portion of the elusive hard simplicities of his lyricism can liquefy like ice. But enough remaining parts to show a writer who changes the normal in obviously common language.

His first assortment of verse '*17 Dikter*' was published in 1954, while he was still at college. He was since thought about his movements in the Balkans Spain and Africa, and analyzed the disturbed history of the Baltic locale through the contention among ocean and land.

Critics have applauded Mr. Transtromer's poems for their accessibility, even in translated version, nothing his rich depiction of long Swedish winters, the cadence of the seasons and the obvious environmental magnificence of the nature.

Transtromer has composed stanza known for its intimate, evocative and in some cases otherworldly depictions of nature and the human mind. For such functions as 'Baltics 'and 'Windows and Stones' in a real sense language pundits have adulated his present for making fine, concentrated perceptions without dodging bigger questions. Later throughout everyday life, he started investigating complex subjects of memory, maturing and demise.

Transtromer's finished works can be found in a single English volume distributed by the New Directions Press, the 288-page "*The Great Enigma*'" which incorporates a short diary he composed after his stroke. Transtromer has occupied a compelling situation in the Swedish writing from the 1950's. In the English talking world he is maybe the most popular present day Scandinavian artist. Standard practice for Transtromer's work is surrealistic imagery; regularly called a poet's poet. His translators include such names as J.Bernlef, Caj Westerberg, Robert Bly, Bei Dao, Joseph Broadsky, and Czeslaw Milosz. His work has step by step moved from the conventional and driven nature verse written in his mid twenties toward a more obscure, individual, and more open verse. His works barrels into the deep darkness, endeavoring to comprehend and wrestle with the mysterious, looking for greatness.

A large portion of Transtromer's verse assortments are portrayed by economy, concreteness and poignant metaphors. In his most recent assortments, *Sorgegondolen* (1996; *The Sorrow Gondola*, 1997) and Den StaraGatan 2004, (*The Great Enigma*, 2006), Transtromer has moved towards a significantly more modest arrangement and a more serious level of fixation. Mr. Transformer cautiously sets up a few interconnecting topics: The demonstration of creation, the challenges of insight and the astounding un-plannable nature of craftsmanship. This is such a verse that regularly offers to easygoing perusers as much as to subject matter experts. Partially in light of the fact that it will in general go over well in interpretation. One of Transformers withstanding interests fixation, nearly is the unpredictable idea of character and the trouble of shielding something so hard to portray or analyze. The inconvenience engaged with seeing oneself or other people, is preceded in later poems like *The Gallery*. Mr.

Transformer has been attracted progressively to haiku that from dearest of so numerous third grade classes.

The structure plays to a significant number of his qualities or strength: economy, pressure, allegorical dexterity and speed. Also, in its capacity to talk uproariously through the littlest of gestures, the haiku fills in as a powerful with discourse since a stroke in 1990.

Chapter Two - A Critical Journey through the Works of Nobel Laureate Tomas GöstaTranströmer

Tomas GöstaTranströmer is a Swedish author, analyst and translator. His poetry catches the long Swedish winters, the cadence of the seasons and the substantial, barometrical magnificence of nature. Transtromer's work is likewise described by a feeling of secret and miracle hidden in the daily practice of regular day to day existence, a quality which frequently gives his poems a strict measurement. In fact, he has been depicted as a Christian poet. Transtromer is acclaimed as one of the main Scandinavian author since the Second World War. Literary pundits have lauded his poetry for its availability, even in translation. His poems have been translated into more than sixty dialects. Transtromer was brought into the world in Stockholm in 1931 and raised by his mom, a teacher, following her separation from his dad. He got his auxiliary instruction at the Sodra Latin School in Stockholm, where he started composing verse. Other than the publications in selected journal publications, his first assortment of poems, *17 Poems* was published in 1954. He proceeded with his schooling at Stockholm University, graduating as a therapist in 1956 with extra studies, in religion, history and writing. Somewhere in the range of 1960 and 1966, Transtromer split his time between functioning as a therapist at the Roxtuna place for adolescent wrongdoers and composing poetry. Transtromer is viewed as one of the most powerful Scandinavian writers of recent years. He distributed a short self-portrayal, *Minnenasermig* (The Memories see me). The two related much of the time, and Bly would make a translation of Transtromer's poems into English. The Syrian writer Adunis assisted with spreading Transtromer's notoriety in the Arab world, accompanying him on readings. In the 1970s, different artists blamed Transtromer for being isolates from his own age, since he didn't manage social and policy centered issues in his sonnets and books. His work exists in and further builds up the Modernist and Expressionist/Surrealist language of twentieth century poetry. His clear, apparently basic pictures from regular day to day existence and nature specifically uncover spiritualist knowledge to the all inclusive parts of the human psyche. Transtromer is viewed as an expert of allegory, meshing incredible pictures into his sonnets absent a lot of adornment.

His works are described by economy, ground-breaking symbolism, and are regularly worked around his own encounters and mixed with his affection for music and nature. Transtromer went to Bhopal following the gas misfortune in 1984, and close by Indian artists, for example, K. Satchidanandan, participated in a verse perusing. His later sonnets are hazier, examining existential inquiries of life, demise and sickness: "Waking up is a parachute jump from dreams". Liberated from the Suffocating choppiness the explorer sinks toward the green zone of morning," peruses the introduction to " *The Great Enigma* ", his last assortment, delivered in Swedish in 2004 and after two years in English: "Things flare up. From the viewpoint of the quivering lark he is aware of the huge root systems of the trees, their swaying underground lamps", Transtromer wrote: "But aboveground there's greenery — a tropical flood of it — lifted arms, listening to the beat of an invisible pump". Other than the Nobel Prize, his distinctions incorporate the Lifetime Recognition Award from the Griffin Trust for Excellence in Poetry, the AftonbladetsLiterary Prize, the Bonnier Award for Poetry, Neustadt International Prize for Literature, the Oevralids Prize, the Petrarch Prize in Germany, the Swedish Award from International Poetry Forum, and the Swedish Academy's Nordic Prize.

Transtromer endured a stroke in 1990, and following a six-year quiet distributed his assortment *Sorgegondolen* (*Grief Gondola*) (1996); this assortment was converted into English by Michael McGriff and MikaelaGrassl as The Sorrow Gondola (2010). He lives in Sweden. Tranströmer turns into the eighth European to win the world's head artistic honor the previous 10 years, following the German author Herta Müller in 2009, the French writer JMG le Clézio in 2008 and the British writer Doris Lessing in 2007. Adulated by the adjudicators for his dense clear pictures, which give us new admittance to the truth, Transtromer's dreamlike investigations of the internal world and its connection to the rough scene of his local nation... Transtromer is not just Scandinavia's most significant artist, he is a writer of world height – and that has at last been freely recognized. Fulton stated that a few writers utilize their own language so thickly they won't decipher by any stretch of the imagination. Transtromer is not one of these. From various perspectives the language he utilizes is moderately unadventurous and basic, he gives individuals irregular pictures which are in some cases exceptionally astonishing and give the peruser a stun. He is expounding on the unavoidable issues of death, history, memory, nature. Individuals are kind of the crystal where all these extraordinary substances meet and it causes us important. The peruser will never to feel little subsequent to perusing the poetry of Tomas Transtromer.

Tomas Transtromer has portrayed his poetry as "meeting places", where dim and light, inside and outside crash to give an unexpected association with the world, history or ourselves. As indicated by the writer the language walks in sync with the killers. Accordingly one should get another dialect. One of the reasons he has been taken up by endless artists, interpreters and perusers is that his verse is general and specific, supernatural and individual. There has additionally been a mixed up sense that he is a simple writer to decipher.

Truth be told, his poetry is exceptionally melodic and multi-layered, with each word or expression having specific reverberation for Swedish perusers now and again numerous affiliations meeting up in his specific selection of words. His initial work was established in the scene of the island where he spent his summers in youth, drawing on the convention of Swedish nature verse. His later work is more close to home, open end loose, mirroring his expansive advantages in movement, music, painting, archaic exploration and characteristic sciences. He has gotten known as a "buzzard poet", a term instituted by an author named LasseSöderberg to communicate how he sees the world from a stature, in a spiritualist measurement, while bringing everything about the regular world into sharp core interest. His sonnets are regularly investigations of the borderland among rest and waking, between the cognizant and oblivious state. His work barrels into the deep darkness, endeavouring to comprehend and wrestle with the mysterious, looking for greatness. In his poem, " *The Outpost* " he stated, "This kind of religious idea recurs here and there in my poems, that I see a kind of meaning in being present, in using reality, in experiencing it, in making something of it". His words were perused by others, while the poet, who is a sharp musician, contributed by playing pieces exceptionally created for him to play on the piano with just his left hand. He has perused at numerous American colleges, frequently with artist and companion Robert Bly. Transtromer has for quite some time been one of the most widely praised artists in Scandinavia. His work draws on characteristic, mysterious and profoundly close to home issues.

Robin Robertson once expressed, "The images leap out from the page, so the first-time reader or listener has the immediate feeling of being given something very tangible". His work was distributed in a few diaries before he distributed his first book of verse, "17 sonnets," in 1954, winning a lot of approval in Sweden. "A ton of extraordinary artists don't do anything other than composing verse", Transtromer's long-term companion, Swedish creator Lars Gustafsson said. "Yet, here you have a man who has buckled down as long as he can remember as an analyst and who has been composing on Saturday evenings and in his extra time, regularly in little, squeezed rooms. Transtromer's most acclaimed works incorporate the 1966 " *Windows and Stones* ", in which he portrays topics from his numerous movements and " Baltics" from 1974. According to Anna Tillgren, "We have waited and waited, we had nearly stopped hoping but still not given up the last strand of hope" for are overpowered. This is the most joyful day ever for huge numbers of us working at the distributing house. Dan Halperin, distributer of Ecco, one of Transtromer's U.S. distributers and an engraving of HarperCollins, additionally invited the honor, saying Transtromer's poetry is one of a kind: thick, rich and totally its own thing.

Tomas Transtromer's poetry collections are thick with the vibe of everyday routine experienced in a particular spot: the dim, overwhelming Swedish winters, the long defrosts and brief paradisal summers in the Stockholm archipelago. He passes on a feeling of what it resembles to be a private resident in the second half of the 20th century. The declaration of Swedish artist Tomas GostaTranstromer as the beneficiary of the current year's Nobel prize for writing has been praised in China, with numerous freely recognizing the essayist who has numerous fans in the nation. In spite of the fact that the overall view might be that Transtromer won due to his ethnicity subsequent to being named a few times in past years, the responses in China was to a great extent sure. Transtromer had visited Beijing in March 2001. Notwithstanding checking driving Chinese essayists, for example, Mo Yan, Yu Hua and Yan Lianke among his fans, ousted Chinese writer Bei Dao, who was assigned for a similar prize previously, is additionally companions with Transtromer and says he has affected his own work expounded on Transtromer in his 2005 book *The Time of Rose*, which incorporated the Chinese author's perceptions about the Swede and other individual artists. The imagery and oddity showed in Transtromer's poems, frequently dependent on everyday life and the normal world, have likewise impacted somewhat another Chinese artist, Li, who deciphers the new Nobel laureate's works into Chinese. Writer Yu Xinqiao stated that transtromer is at last granted the Nobel prize in writing, which is a correct choice worth applauding. "Tomas Transtromer"; The name consistently makes him think about some sort of goliath Transformer, conveying signals from his redoubt in the cold fields west of Stockholm. Until a new stroke, he additionally composed sonnets. Those sonnets are notable to American perusers in the verse world, if quite a world can be said to exist. He actually plays the piano, with one hand. Each writer has a particular music. Among Transtromer's numerous honors are the Neustadt International Prize for The Petrarca-Pries in Germany, The Golden Wreath of The Struga Poetry Evenings, and the Swedish Award from International Poetry Forum. In 2007, Transtromer got an extraordinary Lifetime Recognition Award given by the trustees of The Griffin Trust For Excellence in Poetry.

It is a proportion of his humanism that he visited the survivors of the Bhopal gas tragedy in 1984 well before Vagarth. His compassion for the human condition runs over even in an easygoing experience. Tall, forcing, with a capturing character, Transtromer steps the worldwide scene like a monster. There is an uplifted mindfulness in his verse, a state of honed discernment. The exceptional attribute of all his composing is a definitely pictured feeling of all his poems. Transtromer has an inborn ability to stay on beat and, in the first Swedish, his poems have their very own indisputable music, which ties up with his adoration for music. His poems are constantly highlighting a more prominent setting: one that is tremendous to our ordinary explanation Tomas Transtromer: *Selected Poems*, 1954 – 1986. Altered by previous U.S. Artist Laureate Robert Hass, this determination of more than 100 sonnets gives maybe the best prologue to Transtromer. Here, twelve distinct interpreters, including Hass, make an interpretation of the sonnets into English; it's a decent method to sort out whose interpretations cause you to feel nearest to the 'genuine' or authentic Transtromer. *The Great Enigma: New Collected Poems*. This 2006 assortment of Robin Fulton's reasonable looked at and save interpretations will give you the most complete image of the curve of Transtromer's profession. It's likewise one of the solitary promptly accessible books that show how the sonnets were initially gathered in Swedish. *The Great Enigma* incorporates everything from the shocking adolescent verses distributed in 1952 (17 Poems), to the frightful Baltics, to the late sonnets of The Sad Gondola. His most recent unique work, *The Great Enigma*, was distributed in 2004: "Awakening is a parachute bounce from dreams. Liberated from the stifling choppiness the explorer sinks toward the green zone of morning", peruses the preface to " *The Great Enigma*", his last poetry assortment, delivered in Swedish in 2004, and after two years in English.

For the Living and the Dead

With this new volume of poetry, Tomas Transtromer once again shows out his gift for capturing and grounding the indefinable, glowing details of our modern world. As its title suggests, *For the Living and the Dead* works to bridge the space between those real and unreal elements of life, suggesting that a surprising, redemptive cohesion can exist within a universe of opposition.

The Deleted World

In his 75th year, Tomas Transtromer can be unmistakably perceived as Sweden's most significant poet, however as an author of worldwide height whose work addresses us now with undiminished lucidity and reverberation. Since quite a while ago celebrated as an expert of the capturing, intriguing picture, Transtromer is a writer of the liminal: attracted over and over to limits of light and of water, the limits among man and nature, attentiveness and dream. A profoundly otherworldly yet mainstream, his incredulity about humankind is ceaselessly tested by the relentless recharging intensity of the normal world. His sonnets are revelations established in experience: extra, brilliant reflections that his unprecedented pictures split open-uncovering something abrupt, strange, and life-changing. Tomas Transtromer's *The Deleted World*, for instance, the expression "translations by" has been relinquished for "Versions by Robin Robertson". Indeed in the introduction Robertson states: "In first experience with Imitation" (1962) Robert Lowell opines that 'Boris Paternak has said that the typical solid interpreter gets the strict importance transport misses the town and that in verse tone is obviously everything.

Robertson tells us that Transtromer, "…could not have been warmer". Meaning he might have affirmed of Robertson's endeavours and so do Robertson. It may be on the grounds that in different books of Transtromer, the translations were regularly harder to track down importance. With Robertson's forms the poems are clear, conveying a message of humanity. He places living animals and nature in juxtaposition to one another and their connection. *The Deleted World* contains just fifteen sonnets, and it has been published in the very year as *Collected Poems*. The assortment is worked around a topic, which may be communicated as far as erasure, fleetingness, the slender, moving line among presence and nonappearance. The Swedish scene is portrayed with startling imagery - surprising in itself and furthermore for the manner in which it draws, with pinpoint precision, mental states, political torture, and mysterious. The world, for Transtromer, barely survives. The smallest development of a branch or breath of wind can send it off base, and the danger of annihilation is consistently close. The issue with numerous sonnets that manage any semblance of obscurity, storms, rust, cold, and wore out lights is an inclination to fall into surrendered despairing. Such sonnets regularly brood a ton yet do not do much else. Transtromer does not fall into this snare, somewhat because of his exact perception, and mostly in light of the fact that his sonnets cannot be diminished to a solitary state of mind. They mirror the intricacy of human feeling with unsparing genuineness. They reject bogus expectation and effortlessly won arrangements, as in Black Postcards:

Transtromer discovers trust just from inside the brutal scene he expounds on. Whatever lies past, one can just arrive from here. In certain poems, the entire better one can do is enduring. In *A Winter Night*, dangers rage like the tempest which "puts its mouth to the house/and blows to get a tone", while we accept cover as well as can be expected, apprehensive that the tempest "will blow us empty". Others are more confident, yet trust is not procured without any problem.

The Sorrow Gondola

Transformer's *The Sorrow Gondola*, deciphered by Michael MC Griff and Mikaela Grassl, portrays the writer s own dumbfounded state brought about by a stroke in 1990, while portraying the lives and works of significant figures in workmanship, for example, the authors Franz Liszt and his Son-in-law Richard Wagner. Alone with the topics of quiet and music, the assortment takes its name from Liszt's work La lagner's *gondola*, which was enlivened by Wagner's ailment and demise in Venice. Because of the sublime work of interpreters MC Griff and Grassl, Transtormer's voice itself turns into *the Sorrow Gondola* that is paddling as the millennia progressed old waterways of history and workmanship. The potential for music and expression speaks to the blessing and the craftsman confronted with confusion, as the initial poem "April and Silence", "I'm carried in my shadow/ like a violin/ in its black case". Implications to Greek folklore, the Bible, and later authentic occasions, for example, will and the fall of the Soviet Union, extended the weight of remarkable abilities to the weight of being in force. The lines "earrings dangle like the sword above Damocles" a "king midas/… who turns.. Everything he touches into klagner" and a "Jesus up a coin/with Tiberius in profile/ a profile without love/ power in circulation" aptly express this weight, shared by the poet, for "what happens is always more than we can carry" (The Sorrow Gondola).

Chapter Three - Conclusion - Bits of Knowledge and Mystical Understandings

This project is a journey through the life of Tomas Transtromer, the Nobel Laureate. Even though he had gone through many jobs, his life is full of poetry and music. Transtromer was honoured for his poetry that is filled with imagination and emotion. His poetry is about morality, reality, solitude and redemption.

Before becoming interested in music and painting, he was dreamed of living the life of an explorer while studying at the Sodra Latin School, he started to read and write poetry. His earlier poems were composed in iambic and alcaic meter. Later he has experimented with blank verse and meter, although he has used free verse in *most of his works. Some of his poems took up themes from his travels in different parts of the world.*

In our investigations, we could see that Swedish writer Tomas Transtromer whose basic yet myotical symbolism tends to subjects of nature, history and passing, won the 2011 Nobel Prize. Transtromer has been known as an expert of myoticism who frequently presents a fantasy like cognizance in which time eases back to take into consideration analyzation of the connection between the internal identity and the uncommon pictures [which are] now and again astounding, and give the perusers a stun. No other writer has this quite a bit of significance on the planet. His works are remarkable and understanding. Transtromer cautiously highlights general interconnecting topics such as; the demonstration of creation; the difficulties of perception; and the surprising; and the unplayable nature of craftsmanship. The typical Transtromer poetry is an activity of refined straightforwardness, wherein moderately save language procures astounding profundity, and each word appears to be estimated to the millimeter. He is an obstructively exceptional author whose style is so basic as to stamp most words appear to be vain and pointless. In an official statement, the Swedish foundation that grants the prize, said that Transtromer, who is broadly viewed as one of Sweden's most significant scholars, was perceived, "on the grounds that, through his consolidated, clear pictures, he surrendered new admittance to the real world". His verse is loaded up with feeling and creative mind, but on the other hand is filled with the unforeseen, making his work on occasion both muddling and invigorating. He is an un obstructively life-changing essayist whose style is so straightforward as to make most words appear to be vain and unnecessary. In interpretation a portion of the dangerous hard simplicities of his lyricism can soften like ice, however enough remaining parts to show a writer who changes the customary in clearly common language.

His most popular works are *The Half Finished Heaven* and the *New collected Poem* s. The two of them are unadulterated gold. They are excellent, and he deciphered quite well. Transtromer is a prompt writer.He is a supernatural and visionary yet specific, and individual. He functioned as a therapist for the majority of his life, and such clinician in right is there in the poems. He expounds on the outskirt between the resting and strolling, between the cognizant and oblivious. A large portion of Transtromer's poetry assortments are portrayed by economy, solidness of powerful allegories. The Nobel Prize is viewed as probably the most noteworthy award in writing and is offered uniquely to living scholars. The foundation's decision here and there sparkles warmed discussion among writing specialists. A portion of its past pictures were dark even to writing specialists while others were generally praised writers beautified with various different honors.

Transformer is the first Swedish author since 1974 to be granted the Prize for his two popular works '*New collected poems*' and *Half-finished Heaven*. He is acclaimed as one of the main Scandinavian authors since the subsequent universal war. His sonnets have a quality gives his sonnet a strict measurements surely he has been portrayed as a Christian writer. In spite of the fact that his abstract yield has since decreased, he had just developed a little however acclaimed assortment of section popular in verse. Mr. Transformer cautiously sets up a few interconnecting subjects, the demonstration of creation, the troubles of discernment and the astonishing unpleasurable nature of workmanship. The Feeling of the Relief of Summers is solid. Poems that however they are a lot of organized on the inward life, or self, there are as yet outside qualities, and really these are not many insides in his poems. For transformer's motivation works in the manner that he has the sensation of being in two places simultaneously or staying alert that in a spot that appears to be extremely shut yet that really everything is open.

His Poetry is loaded with storm minutes when he appears to have found himself napping. He opens up colossal region of involvement inside short verse sonnets. His poems portray topics from his numerous movements. He is a Swedish author who at times depressing however ground-breaking work studies topics of nature, disconnection and character behaviour. In October 2011, he was awarded the Nobel Prize in writing.

He has composed more than 15 assortments of verse, huge numbers of which have been translated into English and 60 different dialects. Neil Astley, the manager of Blood hatchet Books in Britain, called Mr. Transtromer, "a magical visionary writer": "His verse is both widespread and specific", Mr. Astley said, "It's unpredictable however direct simultaneously. He's worked for a lot of his life as an analyst, and the work is portrayed by exceptionally solid mental understanding into humankind". Mr. Transtromer's mummy was a school teacher and his papa a journalist, studied literature, history, religion and psychology at the University of Stockholm, graduating in 1956. He briefly worked as a psychologist at a youth correctional facility. His continuing in the United States started to fill in the 1960's. In 1990, Mr. Transtromer endured a stroke that left him generally incapable to talk. In Sweden, the public had been trusting and hanging tight for Mr. Transtromer to win for a long time. His first book of poems, *17 Poems*, put him on the literary guide in Sweden when he was only 23.

Mr. Transtromer is not only a skilled author; he is additionally an entomologist and has a solid association with nature and issues like biodiversity. In an article about Transtromer and creepy crawlies (insects), the writer cheerfully infers that bugs were referenced in no fewer than 21 percent of the 168 poems in one of Transtromer's assortment of poems. He has even got an insect named after him, the "Transtromerstornbagge", found at the island of Gotland recently.

Transtromers poetry collections are regularly worked around his own insight, around a solitary misleadingly plain picture that opens ways to mental bits of knowledge and mystical understandings. Development and change in piece of his graceful scene is observable, yet racial journalists have condemned his dreams of "cosmic peace". His poetry is once in a while filled with the unforeseen, making his work now and again both perplexing and reviving. Scandinavia's most renowned living artist, he has been known as an expert of supernatural quality. He combined his remaining among pundits and different perusers as one of the main writers of his age. He changes the normal in evidently common language. His poems are widespread and are of universal appeal.

Bibliography

Primary Sources

Halpern, Daniel, and Hopewell, eds. For *the Living and the Dead: New poems and a Memoir*. London: Ecco, 1995. Print.

Michael MC, Michael, and Mikaela, eds. *The Sorrow Gondola*. London: Grassl-Kobenhavn, 2010. Print.

Robert Son, Robin. *The Deleted World*. London: Enitharmon, 2006. Print.

Secondary: Electronic Sources

"An Interview with Tomas Tranströmer." *JurnalToddoppuli*, 6 Oct. 2011, jurnaltoddoppuli.wordpress.com/2011/10/06/an-interview-with-tomas-transtromer/.

"In Praise of... Tomas Tranströmer | Editorial." *The Guardian*, Guardian News and Media, 6 Oct. 2011, www.theguardian.com/commentisfree/2011/oct/07/in-praise-of-tomas-transtromer.

"Official website of Tomas Transtromer".8 oct 2011.web.15 Mar 2013 < tomastranstromer.net/ >

"Poetry,poems,bios Bnd more about Tomas Transtromer".22 Dec 2011.web.15 Mar 2013

"Swedish Poet and Nobel Literature Prize Winner Tomas Transtromer Has Died." *The Independent*, Independent Digital News and Media, 23 Sept. 2015, www.independent.

co.uk/news/people/tomas-transtromer-poet-and-nobel-literature-prize-winner-dies-10139791.html.

"Swedish Poet Tomas Transtromer Wins Nobel Literature Prize." Therecord.com, 6 Oct. 2011, www.therecord.com/news/world/2011/10/06/swedish-poet-tomas-transtromer-wins-nobel-literature-prize.html.

"SWEDISH POET WINS 2011 NOBEL PRIZE FOR LITERATURE." *Culturekiosque*,www.culturekiosque.com/nouveau/news/nobel_prize_lit_tomas_Transtromer011.html.

"The Sorrow Gondola by Tomas Tranströmer." *The California Journal of Poetics*, www.californiapoetics.org/reviews/1566/the-sorrow-gondola-by-tomas-transtromer/.

"Tomas Transtromer as a poet".17 oct 2011.web.15 Mar 2013 com/tomas-transtr-mer/>

"Tomas Transtromer on Twitter".23 Nov 2011.web.15 Mar 2013 twitter.com/TomTranstromer>

"Tomas Tranströmer, Nobel Prize in Literature, 2011." *geni_family_tree*, 28 Sept. 2018, www.geni.com/people/Tomas-Transtr%C3%B6mer-Nobel-Prize-in-Literature-2011/6000000014794352876.

"Tomas Transtromer." *Wikipedia*, Wikimedia Foundation, 8 Mar. 2010, en.wikipedia.org/wiki/Tomas_Transtromer.

"Tomas Transtromer-Biographical".9 oct 2011.web.15 Mar 2013 › Nobel Prizes › Nobel Prize in Literature>

"Tomas Transtromer-Wikiquote".23 Nov 2011.web.15 Mar 2013

Lauramachado, /. "Books." *TomasTranströmer*, 28 May 2012, tomastranstromer.us/category/books/.

Memmott, Mark. "Literature Nobel Goes To Swedish Poet Tomas Transtromer." *NPR*, NPR, 6 Oct. 2011, www.npr.org/sections/thetwo-way/2011/10/05/141097584/literature-nobel-goes-to-swedish-poet-tomas-transtromer.

TodayShow. "Factbox: Sweden's Transtromer, Nobel Literature Laureate." *TODAY.com*, 6 Oct. 2011, www.today.com/news/factbox-swedens-transtromer-nobel-literature-laureate-wbna44798972.

Notes

Critical Appreciation Received for the Book from Several Critics in the Literary Scenario

I love this book!! It's so informative! When I glanced through the chapters it's nice to know that the author has made a brief study but informative one on the Swedish writer Tomas Tranströmer and his major works. The book satisfies those who are new to Tranströmer's writings. The language is very simple and well-spoken.

Dr. Rajesh.M

Assistant Professor & Research Guide,

Post Graduate & Research Department of English,

Sacred Heart College (Autonomous)

Thevara, Kochi, Pin -682013, Ph. 09447378587

Email: rajeshmanayil12@gmail.com

rajeshm@shcollege.ac.in

Website: www.shcollege.ac.in

I agree and love the author after I've really enjoyed this book exclusively written on the Nobel Prize winner Tranströmer. First of all, I like to appreciate the author for his skilful research on Tranströmer and second, I recommend the book for them who desire to have a critical journey through Tranströmer and his poetry collections as mentioned in the title. The book of-course throws light on the select oeuvre of Tranströmer.

Dr. Avis Joseph PhD
Professor in English
English Language Center
University of Applied Sciences-Ibra
PB No 327, Ibra 400
Sultanate of Oman

Thank you!! That just made me smile YES! Authors, especially debut ones, need all the love and THEY DESERVE IT!! I know because I too an author. I would appreciate the author of this academic work because as a debutant the author has shown all his enthusiasm towards research in understanding Tranströmer. The book engages by providing a brief glance of Tranströmer's major works.

Dr. Antony Joseph
Assistant Section Officer, Academics
Mahatma Gandhi University
Kottayam, Kerala, India -686560
Phone Number : 7510741394
E-Mail: antoletters@gmail.com